Hello, Family Members,

Learning to read is one of the most important accomplishments of early childhood. **Hello Reader!** books are designed to help children become skilled readers who like to read. Beginning readers learn to read by remembering frequently used words like "the," "is," and "and"; by using phonics skills to decode new words; and by interpreting picture and text clues. These books provide both the stories children enjoy and the structure they need to read fluently and independently. Here are suggestions for helping your child *before, during,* and *after* reading:

Before

- Look at the cover and pictures and have your child predict what the story is about.
- Read the story to your child.
- Encourage your child to chime in with familiar words and phrases.
- Echo read with your child by reading a line first and having your child read it after you do.

During

- Have your child think about a word he or she does not recognize right away. Provide hints such as "Let's see if we know the sounds" and "Have we read other words like this one?"
- Encourage your child to use phonics skills to sound out new words.
- Provide the word for your child when more assistance is needed so that he or she does not struggle and the experience of reading with you is a positive one.
- Encourage your child to have fun by reading with a lot of expression . . . like an actor!

After

- Have your child keep lists of interesting and favorite words.
- Encourage your child to read the books over and over again. Have him or her read to brothers, sisters, grandparents, and even teddy bears. Repeated readings develop confidence in young readers.
- Talk about the stories. Ask and answer questions. Share ideas about the funniest and most interesting characters and events in the stories.

I do hope that you and your child enjoy this book.

—Francie Alexander
Reading Specialist,
Scholastic's Learning Ventures

To Nancy, Karen, Beth, and Tara
G.M.

To Ron Myrtis and Shari,
who know a lot about snow
B.C.

To Richy, Megan, and Michael
G.B.K.

ISBN 0-439-10803-9

Text copyright © 1992 by Bernice Chardiet and Grace Maccarone.
Illustrations copyright © 1992 by Scholastic Inc.
All rights reserved. Published by Scholastic Inc.
SCHOLASTIC, HELLO READER, CARTWHEEL BOOKS
and associated logos are trademarks and/or registered trademarks
of Scholastic Inc.

Library of Congress Cataloging-in-Publication Data available

12 11 10 9 8 7 6 5 4 3 2 1   9/9 0/0 01 02 03 04

Printed in the U.S.A.   24
First printing, December 1999

SCHOOL FRIENDS

The Snowball War

by Bernice Chardiet and Grace Maccarone
Illustrated by G. Brian Karas

Hello Reader! — Level 3

SCHOLASTIC INC. Cartwheel BOOKS®

New York Toronto London Auckland Sydney
Mexico City New Delhi Hong Kong

Bunny wanted to play in the snow all day.
But she had to go to school.

Bunny made footprints in the snow.
First she made a straight line.
Then she made a squiggle.

Thud!
Something hit the back
of Bunny's coat.
It was a snowball.

Bunny turned around.
No one was there.

Bunny saw her friend, Cynthia,
in the schoolyard.

"Can you come to my house
after school?" asked Cynthia.
"Yes," said Bunny. "I'll bring
my Barbie™."
"You're my best friend in the
whole world," Cynthia said.

Raymond was waiting for them
in the classroom.
"I know who threw that snowball,"
Raymond said to Bunny.
"Who?" Bunny asked.
"It was me," said Raymond.
The school bell rang.

"It's time to take your seats. We have
lots to do today," said Ms. Darcy.
The class worked hard all morning.

At recess, Ms. Darcy's class played
"The Farmer in the Dell."
Sam was the farmer,
and Brenda was the farmer's wife.
Brenda picked Cynthia to be the child.

Then Cynthia picked Bunny to be the nurse.
Bunny liked having a best friend!

Raymond was the rat as usual.
Raymond Allen Tally's initials
spelled R.A.T., which was what
most of the kids called him.

R.A.T. picked Martin to be the cheese.

After "The Farmer in the Dell,"
the kids jumped rope.
It was Bunny's turn.
She looked over at Cynthia.

Brenda was whispering in Cynthia's ear.
And she was looking at Bunny.
Bunny wondered why.
Her feet got tangled in the rope.
Cynthia and Brenda giggled.

"What's so funny?" Bunny asked.
"It's a secret," Brenda said.
"Yes, it's a secret," Cynthia repeated.
"And we won't tell you."
"That's not fair," said Bunny. "You're
supposed to be my best friend."

When Ms. Darcy blew her whistle
the boys and girls lined up and
went back to their classroom.

It was still snowing after school.
"I'll get my Barbie™, and then I'll be
right over," Bunny said to Cynthia.
"I changed my mind," Cynthia said.
"You can't come over today.
I'm going to Brenda's house."

Bunny was very sad as she walked home.
Cynthia and Brenda walked ahead of her.
They were holding hands and giggling.
Look at Brenda, Bunny thought to herself.
*She thinks she's a princess with those curls
bobbing up and down.*

Bunny felt a snowball hit her.
She turned around and saw R.A.T.
Why do I have all the bad luck?
Bunny wondered.

On Saturday Bunny went outside
to play in the snow.
Cynthia and Brenda were already
playing in Brenda's yard.
"Hi, Bunny!" Brenda waved.
"Come over and play with us."
Bunny was happy that the girls wanted
to play with her again.

"Hi, Bunny," Cynthia said.
Brenda whispered in Bunny's ear.
"Cynthia is a sore loser. I don't
like playing with her anymore.
Let's hide from her."

Suddenly, Cynthia found herself all alone.
"Where are you?" she called.

Cynthia searched and searched.
She could not find Brenda or
Bunny anywhere.

Cynthia started to cry.
"They don't like me anymore," she said.
And she slowly walked home.

At lunchtime, Cynthia called Bunny
on the telephone.
"Let's be best friends again,"
Cynthia said.
"Brenda is too bossy," Bunny said.
"Let's not play with her," said Cynthia.

"Can you come over?" Bunny said.
"I'll be right there," said Cynthia.

Bunny and Cynthia were making snow
angels when Brenda walked by.
"If you play with Cynthia, you can't
play with me," Brenda said to Bunny.
"We don't want to play with you,"
said Bunny.
"See if I care," said Brenda.

She walked back to her yard
and made snow angels of her own.

Just then Bunny and Cynthia were
both hit by snowballs.
When they looked up, they saw R.A.T.,
Sammy, and Martin.
The boys were safe behind a snow fort.

"A snowball fight!" Bunny yelled.
Bunny and Cynthia ran behind a bush.

Cynthia didn't have good aim.
So Cynthia made the snowballs,
while Bunny threw them.

"We're outnumbered," Cynthia said.
"We need help."
"Brenda's good at throwing snowballs,"
said Bunny. "Should we ask her?"
"Yes," said Cynthia. "I hope she'll come."
"Brenda!" Bunny hollered.
"We need your help!"

Brenda ran over to Bunny and Cynthia.
She had to dodge snowballs all the way.

"You sure do need my help," Brenda said.
Brenda had a strong throwing arm.
First she got R.A.T. Then she got Sammy.
Then she got R.A.T. again.

But the boys were still winning.
They had a giant pile of snowballs.
They didn't have to stop to make more.

"They must have a million snowballs,"
Brenda said.
"They must have been making them
all morning," said Bunny.
"They must have been making them
all week," said Cynthia.

"I have a plan," Brenda said.
"You two stay here. I'll sneak up on
the boys and smash their snowballs!"

Bunny and Cynthia kept throwing.
But it was hard to keep up with the
three boys and all their snowballs.

Then the snowballs stopped coming.
"I did it!" Brenda shouted.
"I destroyed their snowballs."
"You didn't get this one," R.A.T. said.
"I have one more just for you."

As R.A.T. threw the last snowball
at Brenda, she ducked.
The snowball hit Martin.
"Whose side are you on?"
Martin asked R.A.T.

"Let's all be on the same side,"
said Bunny. "Let's all be friends."
"I have an idea," said Martin.
"Let's go to my house for hot chocolate."

And that's what they did.